W9-AZD-059

Also Available
by Bill Martin Jr and Eric Carle

Polar Bear, Polar Bear, What Do You Hear?

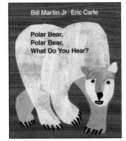

"A visually and aurally splashy work, this is a splendid successor to *Brown Bear*, one that no fan of that popular bruin will want to be without."
—*Publishers Weekly*

Panda Bear, Panda Bear, What Do You See?

★ "Another standout from the creators of a line of perennial favorites."
—*Publishers Weekly*, starred review

The Eric Carle Museum of Picture Book Art was built to celebrate the art that we are first exposed to as children. Located in Amherst, Massachusetts, the 40,000-square-foot museum is the first in the United States devoted to national and international picture book art.

Visit www.picturebookart.org

Henry Holt and Company
Publishers since 1866
175 Fifth Avenue
New York, New York 10010
mackids.com

Henry Holt® is a registered trademark of Macmillan Publishing Group, LLC.
Copyright © 1967 by Holt, Rinehart and Winston;
renewed 1995 by Bill Martin Jr
Text copyright © 2004 by the Estate of Bill Martin Jr
Illustrations copyright © 1992 by Eric Carle
Eric Carle's name and his signature logotype are trademarks of Eric Carle.
All rights reserved.

Library of Congress Cataloging-in-Publication Data available
ISBN 978-0-8050-8797-0 (International paperback edition)
ISBN 978-1-250-17254-9 (Scholastic edition)

First published in 1967 in a slightly different form
by the School Division, Holt, Rinehart and Winston
First general book edition—1983
Newly illustrated edition published in 1992 by Henry Holt and Company

Printed in China by Toppan Leefung Printers Ltd.,
Dongguan City, Guangdong Province

10 9 8 7 6 5 4 3 2 1

Brown Bear, Brown Bear, What Do You See?

By Bill Martin Jr
Pictures by Eric Carle

Henry Holt and Company · New York

Brown Bear,
Brown Bear,
What do you see?

I see a red bird
looking at me.

Red Bird,
Red Bird,
What do you see?

I see a yellow duck
looking at me.

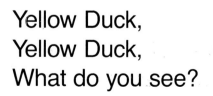

Yellow Duck,
Yellow Duck,
What do you see?

I see a blue horse
looking at me.

Blue Horse,
Blue Horse,
What do you see?

I see a green frog
looking at me.

Green Frog,
Green Frog,
What do you see?

I see a purple cat
looking at me.

Purple Cat,
Purple Cat,
What do you see?

I see a white dog
looking at me.

White Dog,
White Dog,
What do you see?

I see a black sheep
looking at me.

Black Sheep,
Black Sheep,
What do you see?

I see a goldfish
looking at me.

Goldfish,
Goldfish,
What do you see?

I see a teacher
looking at me.

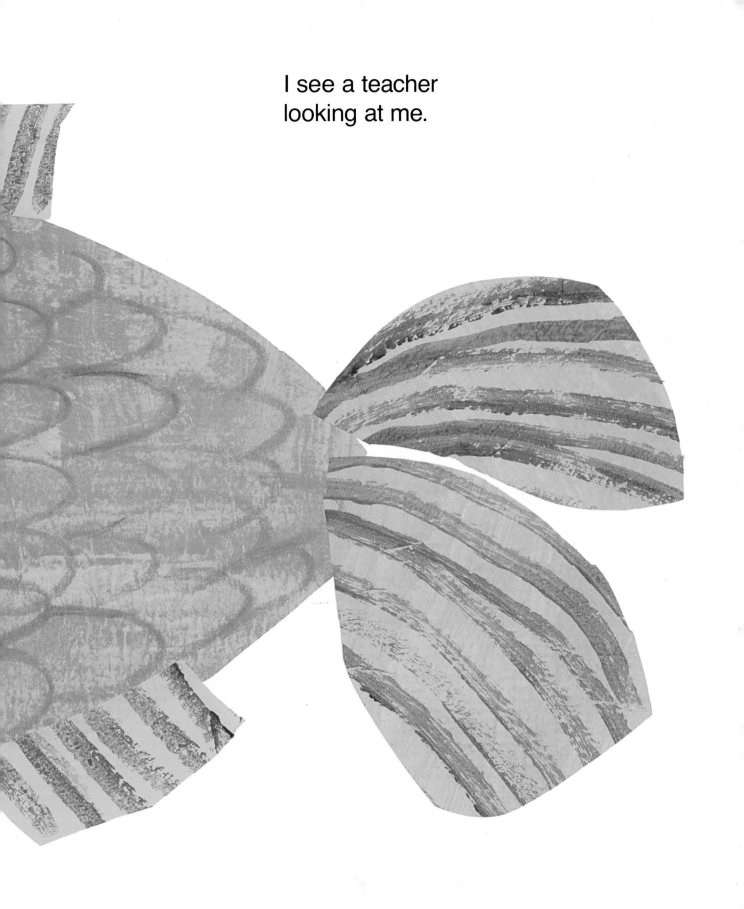

Teacher,
Teacher,
What do you see?

I see children
looking at me.

Children,
Children,
What do you see?

We see a brown bear,

a red bird,

a green frog,

a black sheep,

a goldfish,

a yellow duck,

a blue horse,

a purple cat,

a white dog,

and a teacher
looking at us.
That's what we see.

Kenny Comerford

Bill Martin Jr (1916–2004) wrote children's books for more than thirty years. He earned a Ph.D. in early childhood education and was a proponent of using rhyme and rhythm to teach young children how to read.

Paul Shoul

Eric Carle, the illustrator of many beloved children's books, was born in the United States, but spent his early years in Stuttgart, Germany, where he studied art and design at the Academy of Applied Art. *Brown Bear, Brown Bear, What Do You See?* was the first book he illustrated.